# A Rocky Start

Written by
Anthony Tucker

Illustrations, Cover, and Editing by
Breanne "Cari" Carlson

Self-published

New York, NY, USA

anthony.tucker82@gmail.com
Twitter: @TuckerAnthony
http://www.anthony-tucker.com/

The visual artist Breanne "Cari" Carlson is a professional freelancer open to the public.
Requests for commissions and all other correspondence are always welcomed. You may reach Cari at:
PO BOX 479463,
Chicago, IL, 60647A
(312) 320-3847
cari@sepiarainbow.com
Twitter: @TheSepiaRainbow
http://sepiarainbow.com/
http://sepiarainbow.tumblr.com
http://www.twitch.tv/mixiekins/profile

"Maw" free font © 2013-2016 by Fontm of New York, NY, USA.
Used under the Attribution-NoDerivatives 4.0 International (CC BY-ND 4.0)
http://fontm.com/maw-font/

Ordering Information: Please contact the publisher, Anthony Tucker, at his address above.
Printed in the United States of America,
ISBN 978-0-692-75563-1
First Edition

# Foreword

Growing up in East Harlem wasn't always easy. There were many challenges that I had to overcome in order to become successful in life. I am currently a public school teacher based in the South Bronx, where I taught 5th grade students and Pre-K students. The South Bronx is one of the poorest communities in the country, home primarily to African American and Hispanic families, as reflected in my school. My students have few examples of success stories around them, and rarely read stories in which the characters hail from the same environment.

The main goal for most in an urban setting is to get a job and start making money as soon as possible. There is little to no guidance or focus on building a career. Because I myself was just looking to get a job and start making money, I have tried many different occupations. I quickly found myself bored with them and gave up on them one after the other. It was mostly due to the fact that I wasn't passionate about what I was doing, but once I found the passion to drive myself forward, I quickly learned that that was all that was missing.

I thought that telling my own story to my former students would give them inspiration and motivation to keep going, as I essentially come from the same background as they. I hope this simple yet inspirational story could reach a wide audience of students in the South Bronx and beyond. There are many factors that will test you in life, and to that I say, be strong and keep pursuing your passion.

I dedicate this book to the teachers who never believed in me, to the teachers who did, to my former 5th grade students in the South Bronx for giving me the inspiration to create this story, to my friends and family who have encouraged me to turn this simple story into a picture book, to Breanne Carlson, an incredible artist who brought each page to life with stunning illustrations and was incredibly patient throughout the entire process, to my wife, who frequently listened to my uncertainty on many occasions and provided me with positive reinforcement, and to my daughter Aniya, who provided me with the will to be the best me I can be since 2005.
Thank you all.

Anthony Tucker

There was a young boy
who grew up in a place very similar to the South Bronx.

This place is called East Harlem.

This young boy was great at anything he attempted, but he was never committed.

The young boy would start something and would never finish.

He would start his homework and would never finish.

He would start a race and would never finish.

He would even start telling a joke, but he would never finish

He was good at everything,
but the thing he was best at...

Date: 10 December

(F)

Finish Your work!

was never finishing anything

Even when he grew up
things didn't change.

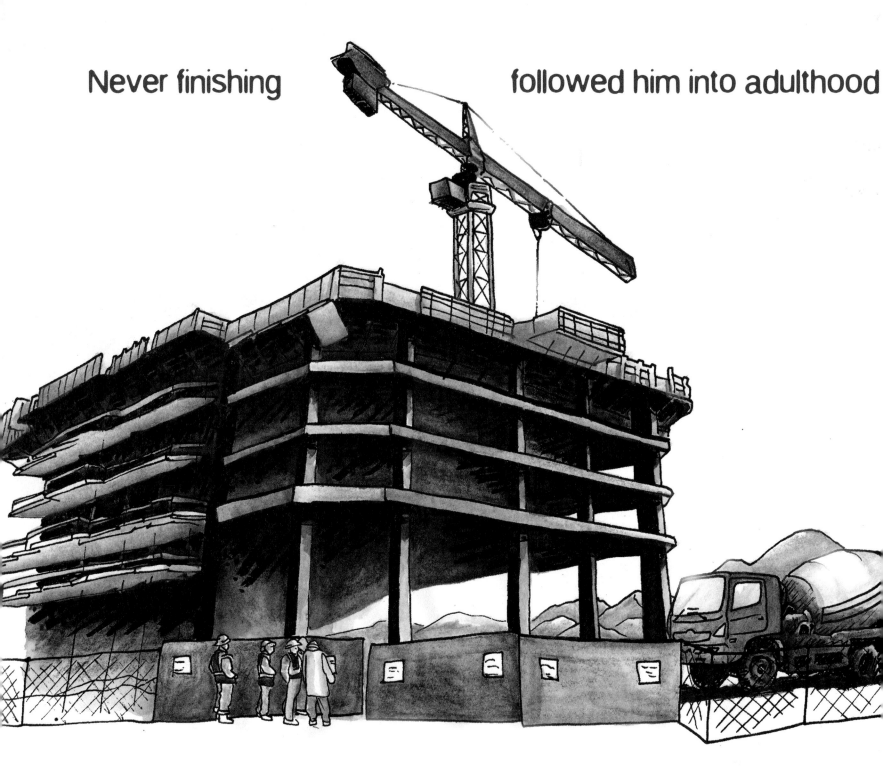

He began to work in construction, but never finished a building.

He became a barber, but never finished a haircut.

Until he realized he hadn't found his passion.

The first hint of inspiration came while he was hanging out on the block.

He noticed a boy wearing a backpack, and found out he was on his way to college.

He thought that he too could do that. Even though he was a bit discouraged because he never finished anything, he set a goal to be the first in his family to accomplish this one thing.

He began college, and he did finish.

So he wanted a job to help others finish things.
That's when another hint of inspiration came.

A subway ad read

That's when he knew that he wanted
to do something meaningful
and help others find their passion.

And that's what he did,
he became a teacher, and now
he always finishes what he starts.

# A Letter from the Artist

First, thank you so much for not only picking up this book, but also reading it! I'm elated to know that this is going to be in the hands of li'l tykes, this is the exact kind of book I wish I had when I was small. There's a lot of weird things about being young, though you tend to only realize it when you're older.

When you're little, one of the weirdest things is seeing people much older than you are, like teenagers or adults. Know what I mean? They all seem so much bigger and older, almost like they're entirely different creatures. Well, similar enough. Maybe as different as cats and dogs are-- they both walk on four legs, but they seem so different!

It's pretty hard to imagine yourself as an adult, and for me, I couldn't picture it one bit. I'd try to think of what it would be like when I could drive a car, or have a job, but I kept drawing a blank. (In fact, I found it so impossible to imagine, that when my friends all said they had no trouble picturing their future selves, I was sure this just meant I had no future, that I was destined to die young or something!) All I could really imagine was what I already knew, like slight variations of my past experiences.

Time seemed to take ages to pass, too. Especially if there was something like a birthday to count down to. Torture! Every summer vacation seemed as though time was standing still until, suddenly, one day you find out school starts back up the next week! "NOOOOO! There was so much I wanted to do!" I'd waste time doing things in the present, and being unable to imagine the future, so I'd start reflecting on the past. I'd stay up way too late, worthlessly laying in bed, in the dark, spacing out at the ceiling. My mind was always humming with contemplation on the past and how a scenario might have played out if this-or-that happened some other way.

It often felt like I was floating through a stagnant dream, in stasis, but it didn't really bother me. I'd do whatever it was I did each day, usually drawing. I couldn't imagine the future, so I'd just extrapolate from things I'd see. If I wanted to draw something I'd ever seen, I'd look up similar examples (like lizards if I wanted to draw a dragon). I was sure I'd always keep drawing, it was the only thing that ever truly made me happy; since I was always making so much art, I assumed I'd become an artist some day.

Well, unlike Anthony, I didn't really grow up to be someone terribly useful. Art was something that made me different from almost everyone else I knew, but when I graduated from high school, college was too expensive, and didn't even guarantee I'd get a job as an artist. So, I got a job doing Technical Support for websites. I did that for almost 10 years, and hated it. I kept doing it to pay the bills so I could do my little art projects at the end of the day. Well, until work got so intense that I was too tired to do any art.

After a few years of literal "all work and no play, " I was finally able to see myself in the future. I pictured myself being unfulfilled, dying as a lonely, sub-par, stressed-out IT Rep, with a suitcase of really lame old sketches as my legacy. When I eventually die, my life's work would probably just rot in a closet until somebody threw it out. Luckily, about half a year ago I lost my most recent tech job. I tried taking a stab as a freelance artist, and wouldn't you know it, Anthony was one of my first clients! (Thanks, man!) I've been working with him, and a bunch of other clients, for these past 6 months and have never been happier.

I just hope that, if you can ever see your future self and don't like what you see, you give something else a try. If there's something you do all the time that makes you truly happy, try as hard as you can to do it!

Breanne "Cari" Carlson